MY MOTIVATION

BY

KIM L. WALTON

Table of Contents

Dedication

This book is dedicated to my family who inspires me in so many ways. Thank you, to my in-house editors and advisors Ernest, Rose, Danjanec, Michael, and, of course, my wonderful Aunt Helen Simmons co-owner of Creative Woodworking for taking the time to read this book and offer sincere advice.

I am so blessed!

MY MOTIVATION

Foreword

Twenty-one-year- old college student, Sandra Walts, finds helping others to be the motivation she needs to help her earn a better education. Sandra thought she was ready for the rigors and hard work that go along with being a college student and working full time.

She had no idea that staying motivated may be the most difficult thing she has ever had to do. In a blink of an eye, Sandra's world will be turned upside down when she has to face both mental and physical abuse. Will she give up on achieving her dreams and her desire to help others?

Or, will she fight through the pain and disappointment and continue struggling to find the one thing that she can indeed call "My Motivation."

ISBN-13:978-0-9976138-0-3 (eBook)
ISBN-13:978-0-9976138-1-0 (print edition)

Copyright © 2015 Kim L. Walton
Book Cover and Design by Kim L. Walton
Published by: Kim L. Walton
First Edition: January 2016

Memories

This was to be just another Friday night studying and sleeping. Instead, I ended up hanging out with friends and seeking that so-called good time.

"Hi, my name is Sandra. I hope you enjoy the story I am about to tell."

I needed and wanted to write it down. For those who find themselves in my situation. Those who need to know that the struggle is real for many of us. Also, that anyone can survive and overcome their struggles.

The right motivation can come from anything, change does not mean the end; rather it signifies a new beginning.

I was anticipating a long weekend ahead of me, between homework and my job. I saw myself hunched over an old scarred desk with a mug of black coffee to keep me going. I never thought that going to school would be this hard.

Currently, I attend Southside Community College, a small college on the outskirts of Meherrin Virginia. In six months' I will have completed my Associate's degree in Healthcare Administration.

From there my plan is to transfer to a four-year college and obtain my Bachelors in Healthcare Administration. My goal and passion are to become a registered nurse with my very own company.

More like an agency! I have always wanted to help people, starting my own business will be the second step in achieving that goal. The first, of course, is to finish school with my degree.

I hear a knock on my door. It interrupts my thinking process. My current boyfriend Keith stands there with a big smile on his face. Keith and I have been dating for two months' now, and I was really feeling him. He has such a beautiful smile and kind eyes.

He also has a little jelly roll around his middle. His middle feels all soft and fluffy. Why do I like that roll? It just seems real for a guy/man to have the same problems losing weight that we women go through. Anyway, I like the roll, and it makes me smile just to feel it.

Keith tells me "Drop those books and pencils, over-achiever, and let's go out tonight."

Laughing, I tell him "no" that I have a paper due Monday.

"Besides, Keith, I have to work six hours at the clinic tomorrow, as you already know," I explain to him.

"Please, Sandra," Keith says.

"Hanging out with you and the party gang tonight will only slow me down with completing my class assignments and my focus on work tomorrow.”

“Come on Sandra, one night out will not change that grade point average. I will take you to work tomorrow and pick you up, plus buy breakfast and lunch tomorrow if you go,” Keith states.

He takes my hand and twirls me around the room, and starts to sing, “When somebody loves you back,” one of my favorite songs by the great Teddy Pendergrass.

Yep, I am a sap, between that song and him singing. My fingers started to snap, and hips began to roll. Yeah, I was going. *Dang, where does my backbone go when I need it to keep me on track?*

When I think back on that conversation, I wonder what would have changed. Had I not went out that night? Probably nothing, but I will always wonder.

When Keith approached me two months ago, I have

to admit that I was shocked, and a little cautious. I just kept thinking: *what could this good-looking man, want with me?* Now don't get me wrong, I am not putting myself down. However, I was surprised and taken aback by his attention.

I am five feet, ten inches, tall and weigh two hundred pounds give or take a few pounds. Do not get me wrong, this weight looks good on my frame. I do not stress about it. I eat right, exercise, and dress this body well. I realized back in high school that I would never be a size eight, so I make sure that my size fifteen/sixteen is healthy.

"Baby, you listening?" asked Keith.

I really do like him, but I am also serious about my education. After tonight I will talk to him and get him to understand what this truly means to me.

"Keith, I will go this time, but I need to be in early so that I can finish my paper," I say to him.

"Also Keith, my mom and grandmother want me to come home for dinner tomorrow."

"Okay, baby I will have you home early, be ready by six beautiful," Keith said.

He gives me the sweetest kiss as he leaves. As he is going out the door, my roommate Sheila comes in. Sheila is well put together. What the guys/men call a brick house. At least that is what people say when she walks by. She is so curvaceous, yet, so short. It is like looking at Angela Basset at five foot five.

The thing about Sheila is, she believes her body is just average. When a brother steps to her the wrong way, she walks. She says that she wants a man who appreciates her mind first and the body second. I guess that is why we are friends. I can relate to feeling like a piece of meat to someone.

" Sheila, are you going out with the gang tonight?" I asked.

"Yeah, I just saw Ralph and he already asked me" Sandra."

"Would you jump him, Sheila, if you could?" I asked her.

"Who, Ralph?" Sheila asked with a dreamy look.

"Yeah, Ralph, meathead," I say to her.

"Sandra you are too funny, I would, but I do not want to appear fast and scare him off."

"Girl you are in for a surprise with him."

"What do you mean, Sandra? Do you know something that I do not?"

"Listen, Sheila, during these last few months,

whenever we hang out. Ralph is right there with you, beside you, behind you, always with you."

"Okay, I am still confused and do not get you? Sandra?"

"Well, his actions tell me that he is interested in you. Sheila, I think that he is waiting for a sign from you that you feel the same."

"Girl, if you see all that then I am jumping on his hot ass tonight!"

I found myself laughing at what Sheila said about Ralph. If she ever gave him the sign, he would be all over her faster than she could get to him. Ralph has been the only guy at school that I have seen Sheila show interest in. That says a lot about my home-girl and what she stands for!

"Girl, what are we wearing tonight?" I asked Sheila.

She loves clothes, whenever we are about to party with the gang, I let her choose what I wear. We always look tight with whatever she chooses anyway. Sheila lays out for me a long sea blue skirt with a lace camisole to go with it, and a matching sea blue jacket. For the shoes, she chooses a pair of low-heeled sandals that have blue rhinestones on top of them.

"I like your choice for me, but what are you wearing?" I asked her.

"Sandra, you know that when we go out together the sisters have to match a style correctly."

She pulls out a long, vibrant red skirt for herself. The matching camisole hot red jacket makes the skirt pop. As we rush around getting ready for tonight doing our makeup and hair for each other.

I ask her if two months is too soon to have sex with a

person. Well, it has been almost three months.

As I am telling her that, I think that I am ready to have sex with Keith. Shelia does what a good friend should do by asking, are you sure about this?

"Sandra, I know that you have been dating him for a few months now. Why the rush? Is he pressuring you to have sex?"

"No sis it is nothing like that. I honestly do want to be with him. I think that I am ready now."

"Sandra, I just do not want you to let him or anyone else pressure you into something you're not ready for."

"Keith has been so patient with me never going too far, Sheila. He seems to understand that I needed to take my time."

I lost my virginity at fourteen, and I can honestly say that I hated every minute of it. I even stayed with the person through just about all of my high school years. Because it was expected of me and everyone else was doing it during that time.

I hated having sex with him. For one thing, I was too young, naïvely listening to those so-called friends say 'everybody is doing it.'

Some would ask, "Are you chicken? Do you think you better than we are?" I realized then that something was wrong. Nevertheless, I just did not know how to fix it. Admittedly, I was scared to lose friends or who I thought were friends. Now I know that they were not my friends!

If they were, they would have respected my decisions, thoughts, and opinions.

Kids or teenagers who start having sex early have no idea of the consequences of their actions. The risk he or she takes with their lives. In my opinion, sex at that young age only causes pain and confusion. As my granny would say, 'you have no clue what you are doing!'

I was lucky, though. No babies had come from me doing that grown-up act. I did have enough sense to protect myself at least. I used to go get condoms from the free clinic back home all the time. I did have enough sense to force my ex to use them. Now at twenty-one and soon to be twenty-two years old I think that I am ready to experience grown up sex.

"Sheila, I have feelings for Keith. No, I do not believe it's love. At least, I do not think so, but I do like him and would like to have that experience with him."

I am older now and more educated about sexual intercourse. I tried to explain to Sheila my feelings about having sex with someone you want or are attracted to. And not doing it based on peer pressure or because you're young and dumb.

"Damn Sandra how old are you really, to be this deep and wise about sex?"

"Sheila, I am not that deep, nor that wise. I just feel that, as a grown up, I will be doing it with my eyes open and full of knowledge as they say."

"True, but be really sure, this is serious."

"Sheila, from what I have read, when you do it with someone you like, the experience is so much better. And I want that good feeling that I read about. Yes, I believe in romance and want my toes to curl and my breath to catch!"

On our way out the door, I turned and grabbed the condom that Sheila had given me. I do not know if I am prepared to go all the way mentally. However, it is better to be safe than sorry. I have come so far and do not want to be stupid now or make a life-changing mistake!

On our way downstairs to meet up with the guys, we run into Keith's ex-girlfriend Gloria.

"That girl gets on my damn nerves," Sheila says. "Why is she always getting in your face, Sandra?"

The girl in question is Gloria. She dated Keith before my time. I have never asked him why they broke up. What he did or did not do before he met me is not my business.

I had heard through school gossip that the chick was a straight ho, and that is why he ended the relationship.

As I said, I do not know and have never asked. I feel that it is none of my business. She, however, wants it to be my business. Every time she sees me the chick snarls like a pit-bull and rolls her nose like it is a snout, you know a pig's nose.

We both currently live in the same building, which

makes it hard to avoid the bitch. There are apartment complexes for students to rent while in school. The complexes are about a ten-minute walk from the main campus.

Student tuition payments can go towards housing of course. You also have many private pay students who live in the complexes as well. It is nothing to see groups of students walking to the school campus from the apartment complexes. The prices are also fair for the area, and the rooms are very spacious.

Shelia and I currently rent a two bedroom, two baths with a small kitchen and living room. This college is the only one around and a blessing to those like me.

Back to this crazy woman, Gloria, and her issues. I will not lie Gloria always getting in my face is testing my nerves on a dangerous level. I do not know what to do about it! I do not want the trouble she brings with her presence. Nor am I willing to get myself kicked out of school for fighting.

If I catch a charge of assault, my ass may end up in jail. What would that accomplish in the end? Absolutely nothing! Now I am human there are times that I want to say fuck it, and swing on her ass.

Nevertheless, I hold back, remembering the track I have laid out before me. So I have to be a grown up here.

Besides, my grandmother would be so disappointed in me if I messed up now.

Gloria always has a posse with her. Yep, Pitbull, and her posse would jump my ass if they could. That is another reason why I stay calm. Nanny did not raise no fool, I know the odds are against me.

Her posse is composed of those weak-minded little

girls. Females who need someone to guide them to destruction. I do not think that I have ever heard one of them say anything. Unless it was to repeat whatever it was she was saying. It's just sad. You know they all go to the bathroom together.

"Well, if it's not miss nothing all dressed up to go nowhere," said Gloria.

Okay, here come the insults from piggy snout.

"Aw, cat got your tongue?" Gloria says. "Ya'll know this fat bitch think she has a date with my man."

Now If I had psychic powers I would trip her, and she would fall on her face losing all of her front teeth. I bet that would keep that mouth closed.

"Poor, poor Sandra you do not get it that Keith does not actually want you," Gloria thunders at me.

"Keep walking Sandra she is not worth it," Sheila

says as she pulls me along.

"You step off, wannabe, and leave him alone I am not going to tell you again," Gloria says as she gets all in my face.

"Have mercy, Gloria Keith came to me. Sorry, not the other way around?" I tell her.

"Bitch, you threw your fat-ass at him," Gloria chimes.

"Gloria, get out of my way, I am not in the mood for your stupid ghetto ass tonight."

"Little girl, who the hell do you think you are talking too?" Gloria says while poking me in the chest with her finger.

We were so distracted with each other, neither of us noticed that Keith had come in.

"Gloria, you and your dogs had better get the hell

away from her right now!" Keith yells.

"Keith, she started it," raves Gloria

"Of course, I did," I say turning to Keith "I so want her ignorant ass following me around cussing, threatening, and harassing me," I tell him.

Gloria tries to grab Keith's arm.

He snatches his arm away and tells her to just leave him the hell alone.

"Keith, if you just talk to me we could work this all out," Gloria tells him.

I must be invisible. This dumb chick has seems to have forgotten, that I'm here and that he is not with her anymore.

"Gloria stop this, you're making a scene," says Keith.

"Keith baby, please you know you want me. Your fat friend is the problem," Gloria said to him.

"Keith, I'm ready to go," I tell him while placing my hand on his arm.

"Sandra, you fat bitch, you hear me talking to my man?" Gloria thunders.

"Gloria, you are sad, pathetic, and have no pride. You want to fight me because he came to me? How stupid are you?"

"Sandra, I got this," Keith tells me in a harsh voice.

"Gloria, everything that happened between us was between us. Not you and Sandra. Leave her alone. Stop harassing her for no reason. It is time for you to move on. I have. We are through with each other," Keith tells her.

"Keith, after all we have shared that's how you gonna do me?" Gloria says to him through her tears.

"Gloria, I do not want you back. Keith tells her.

"Why the fuck would I want a girl who gives the ass up to

any and everyone?"

"Hold on Keith, that is not how it went and you know it" Gloria states.

Keith tells her, "Wait, you right. You get mad, drunk, or whatever then go share with anyone that will have it, right?"

"Keith, that is not fair I am not a damn whore, and you know it!" states Gloria.

"Ouch," Sheila just elbowed me in the side.

"What are they talking about Sandra?" Sheila asked.

"Girl, I do not know. Something bad must have gone down," I whisper to Sheila.

"Sandra, she is crying and looking scared. You sure you do not know?"

"Sheila, again, I do not know I have never asked about their relationship. So stop asking me."

"Well hell, Sandra, my nose is itching, so this must be something big," Sheila says.

"Sheila, if you do not!!"

"Okay, okay yes, I am nosey Sandra," Sheila tells me grinning.

Sheila and I watched Keith walk up to Gloria and say something to her, which made her cry even more.

At this point, I am not sure what is going on. But I agree with Sheila, those two went sour real bad and in a bad way.

Keith grabs Sheila and my arm and basically pushes us out the damn door. We can hear Gloria screaming and crying, even after the door closes behind us.

A part of me feels sorry for her right now. Whatever he just said to her must have been hurtful from the expression on her face!

"Sandra, I am so sorry that she keeps bothering you," Keith says.

"Keith look, I think you need to talk to her. I am tired of her, but I am not gonna blame you for her harassing me," I tell him.

"Sandra, I am sorry. I broke up with Gloria long before we met. So none of this should be happening to you."

"You know what Keith? Let's just leave this drama here where it belongs. We made plans for tonight, right? Let's get to them."

"Amen to that. Let's go have fun tonight and enjoy ourselves," Sheila shouts throwing her fist in the air.

As we walk across the apartment complex parking lot I see his boys Ralph, Mike, and my other girlfriend Candace already in his ride.

"I see we are riding in your hummer tonight," I say to Keith.

Placing his arm around my waist, he leans in and says "Yeah, I figured let us ride out in style tonight."

MY MOTIVATION

Party Time

Keith currently works for one of the nightclubs in Keysville VA. He is a bartender and sometimes bouncer. His dream is to own his own club one day. We all have dreams right? Without them, where would we be?

I know some of the people on campus wonder where he got the money to buy a Hummer. A ride like this is something you fantasize about buying one day, right? I know that for a twenty two year old, it is a big something.

Do I really know where he got the money to buy this hummer? Of course not, I have only known him for a couple of months. I hope everything is legit.

He told me that he left and went to the army when he was eighteen and stayed in for four years. When he came out. He had a plan and that was college and the reserve. Between school, the club, and the reserves, he is busy. I just cannot see him having time to hustle.

As he helps me into the front seat, I asked Keith "Why are all of you wearing camouflage tonight?"

"Oh yeah, we have to train this weekend. I figured that I would see my baby this evening, and then leave with my boys later for camp Sandra."

I am looking at him thinking that earlier he did say that he would take me to work and pick me up. So what happened to him just telling me the truth then?

That he had reserve duty this weekend, I would have understood. I do not know if it is the situation or me being paranoid. I feel deceived. Why the lie? Even a small lie in this situation is stupid.

Make me wonder more about a person. Some shit not worth lying about, so why do it?

"No problem lets hit the club and have some fun," I tell him with a straight face.

I am thinking there's no need to spoil the fun for everyone else, and I am already out here now anyway. Our little group screams "Yeah," you know we all about to break out into Usher and Little John's song "Yeah Yeah Yeah."

I speak to Mike and Ralph, then turn and say to my girl Candace that I love the outfit she is wearing tonight.

"Sandra, you know if I am hanging with you and Sheila my shit has to be tight, right?"

"Yeah, okay, Candace. We three will be the finest chicks in the house," I say to her.

"Sandra, girl thanks for the love. My off the rack stuff is nothing compared to yours. Nevertheless, I do try girl, I do try."

Candace believes that I shop at high price outlet stores. Now that is so far from the truth, and laughable really. It just shows that she really does not know me.

I am a bargain shopper. I get it from my grandmother. Bargain shopping is an excellent way to save. I have found some truly good stuff. I hit the thrift store and Goodwill stores all the time. I go at least once a month.

Hell, I have Sheila doing the same thing. We were able to hook our place up, and I mean with good stuff, and we both are able to save some money. We need money for the purchases of cars, schoolbooks, or any other expenses that may come up.

Buying discount clothes and other items is a smart move. Besides, there is no shame in my game. I have never needed to keep up with the Jones' as they say.

On to the club we go. Ghana's is a little nightclub that everyone loves. The club is located on a major highway. Anyone traveling over the weekend on that road can see the lights, hear the music, and stop in for a visit. The club welcomes many new visitors this way.

I noticed as we were pulling in that the parking lot was filling up fast. It was only seven in the evening.

This lets you know that people love the spot. Everyone tries to get in early for parking and a table for dinner upstairs. Around nine or ten at night, you go downstairs and work that food off. Ghana's has a nice size dance floor and a good DJ working the music.

The dance floor is always crowded, and the drinks are not watered down. This club is friendly and well run by its management team. They offer good music, good food, and, of course, good fun.

Since I have been coming to Ghana's nightclub, I took notice that they did not have a problem with all the fighting and gang banging like some of the other nightclubs.

This I can appreciate. Going out should be fun. We should not have to run and duck for cover just to dance.

Fridays are for the twenty-one and over crowd. Saturdays are for the over twenty-five and Sundays is for the thirty plus. Therefore, the club has something for everyone.

As we go in, there is no cover charge. Keith works for them so we all can get in free. Keith leads our group inside and downstairs where the music is playing. We find a booth available that can seat us all towards the back.

"What do you all want to drink and eat?" asks Keith, "I am taking orders now."

We all give our orders to Keith, and he goes to place them for us.

Keith said that we could eat downstairs because we are with him. Normally they prefer guests to eat upstairs. I understand this. Who wants grease from a burger or hot wing sauce all over the dance floor?

Right away Candace and Mike hit the floor dancing grooving to the music of Ice Cube. Dude is one of my favorite rappers. Sheila, Ralph, and I sit at the table talking about nothing important. Just chilling waiting for our food and drinks to arrive.

Lord I love this song, "We Be Clubbing." It makes you want to move.

I am doing the stinky leg under the table and rolling my shoulders ready to jump up when Keith finally arrives with our food and drink orders. Ghana's makes some of the best burgers in the area.

Around ten, I am not going to lie my tail was toasty

and tipsy. I am on the dance floor grinding, the air; yeah, alcohol can get some of us like that. When who comes up to me, but Blake, my old high school boyfriend, and wraps his arms around me.

"Do not do that Blake."

"Old friends cannot dance with each other Sandra?"

"No, we cannot dance with each other. When did we become old friends Blake?"

"Calm down Sandra. The last time I saw you it ended badly, and I wanted to say how sorry I am."

"Look, whatever Blake I am just not trying to go down this road with you."

"Sandra, I just wanted to dance with you. I honestly was not going to try anything else, nor will I cause you any drama or make a scene."

"Blake, I am here with friends and want to enjoy

myself. I have no desire to talk or see you."

"Sandra, you know that I still have feelings for you."

"Of course, you do Blake. You always were good at catching feelings when you did wrong!"

"I made mistakes when we were kids Sandra. Hell, everyone does you know! Have I learned from them? Hell yeah I have."

"Blake, I have learned from my mistakes as well. Therefore, I am telling you that I choose not to talk to you."

"Sandra, I want your forgiveness for all that I did to you. Can we please go somewhere and talk?"

Oh Lord is what I am thinking. This fool is high and will probably beat the living daylights out of me, or worse kill me, in his drug induced state.

"Blake, I am going to walk away now I do not want

to talk, go anywhere, or do anything with you."

"You owe me the chance to make this right, Sandra," the fool says to me as he grabs my jaw.

I learned as a teen that you cannot fight crazy, and when crazy is high, you are literally fucked.

I looked up behind Blake, and there stood Keith looking mad as hell. I was so glad to see him at that moment, I would have given him anything. I see Mike and Ralph also flanking Blake. He did not even know they were there. Thank God for friends who know when to intervene.

Keith steps around Blake and says to me "I let you on the floor by yourself and you in trouble already! What you doing Sandra, flirting and hugging up on another man?"

I give Keith a look as if to say, You are joking, right?

"Ah," Blake says, "the new boy toy. Keith, right? You can go, Sandra and I are just talking."

Keith turns and looks Blake up and down.

"Well, Blake, seeing as I am the man she is currently dating. I think that yall's conversation has lasted long enough."

"Look, man, I had her first in every way. Even popped that cherry, so what you getting is all that I have taught her," Blake thundered.

"Blake it wasn't much, so you must not be a good teacher," Keith says.

"What, did you both forget that I was here?" I said to them both.

We were all making a scene as it was, and if the music stopped. It would just get worse with strangers hearing us argue. Damn, the tension was so thick in here.

You could probably write your name in the air for people to read.

I could tell from Keith's face that he was genuinely angry. I had never seen him look like this not even when his ex-pissed him off.

"I am going to leave and try to talk to you at a later time Sandra," Blake says.

"Let me know when this conversation is supposed to happen, Blake," Keith tells him.

"You better watch your back boy," Blake says as he points his finger at Keith.

"Yeah, that is what you so called tough guys say all the time Blake" Keith shot back at him.

I placed my hand on Keith's arm and told him, "Let it go, and let him go please."

Jerking his arm away, Keith growls at me,

"Whatever, That punk would sneak at a man's back first anyway." Then he walks up to Blake.

"Blake, or whatever your name is you want a piece of me? Then just swing, man, that is all you have to do," Keith taunts him. "However, you and I know what is going to happen when you do. Right BLAKE?"

"Get out of my face!" Blake yells.

"Blake, you sound mad you probably want to pull a gun about now. Bitches like you would not have no fight unless you strapped," Keith taunts him.

"Sandra, let's go. He is not worth my time and energy," Keith said.

I can say that I have never seen anyone back Blake down, especially with just words. He bullied everyone while we were in high school.

Now I am looking at Keith. Not with admiration, but

with a little apprehension. True, I am happy that he helped me avoid that confrontation, but not what he said about me. As if I asked for this trouble! Plus, I am not cool with the sex comment. We have never had sex, why say something so disrespectful and a flat out lie at that?

My grandmother always told me to listen to my gut. Right now, it is telling me that something was wrong with that statement coming from him. Do I try to talk to him now about it? On the other hand, maybe I should wait and see if he brings this mess back up. I do not know what to do!

As we go back to the table, a slow jam comes on. I ask Keith if he would like to dance. I was hoping to get us back on track, at least for tonight.

Keith turns to me and states, "I promised your girl Candace a dance."

"You did what?" I said to him.

"I promised her a dance. Why don't you go sit and enjoy your drink while I keep my promise?"

"You promised a dance on a slow song to my friend, then tell me to sit and have a drink. But you do not see a problem with this?"

"No, I do not see a problem dancing with one of your friends. She has danced with everybody, and I did tell her that I would dance with her before the night was over, Sandra."

Well like a good little, you know the word I sat and had my drink while my so-called boyfriend took another woman onto the floor and slow-dragged with her. How stupid am I?

Mike came to the table and looked at me a little funny. He looked at Keith and Candace on the floor and looked at me again.

"Yeah, I know I am one dumb individual," I said to Mike.

Finally he said while shaking his head, "Go on and drink that drink. You look like you need it, Sandra."

After a couple, minutes of silence, Mike says to me, "You ever hear people say that not everyone is your friend?"

"Why would you say that?" I asked him.

"Sandra, seeing old boy on you pissed Keith off, and he is handling it the wrong way," Mike tells me.

"Mike, I get that, but it's not like I invited Blake on the floor with me. So is this his way of...of what, punishing me?"

"Sandra, I do not think he is thinking straight. Keith probably wants to make you jealous or something."

"Mike, jealousy is not the emotion that I am feeling right now."

"Sandra, I get it. Just remember that your friend there is allowing him to use her to make you mad as well. To me, that speaks volumes about her as a person. Again, I say not everyone is your friend...or boyfriend."

"MIKE, what the fuck are you saying? Do I need to know something?" I yell at him.

"Sandra, sometimes those that smile in your face and laugh with you are actually laughing at you and stabbing you in the back. You dig?"

But what does that mean? My mind is in overdrive. Shit was rolling around in there like mad! What makes Keith think it's okay to play with me this way? What made him think that I would be cool with this shit? I finished my drink and decided to go to the bar and get another.

"Mike, you want another drink or something to eat?"

"Nah shorty, I am good I already have a buzz. That is all I need for now," he tells me.

I get up and head to the bar, looking at the dance floor. Where the hell are they? I realized that I did not see Keith or Candace right away. I got a clearer view of them when I went up to the bar. I knew that I would not be having sex with him tonight. I probably would not have a boyfriend after tonight either.

I decided to get a soda and pretzels. No more alcohol for me tonight. As I wait for my order, I stare in disbelief. Those two trifling muther- somethings, are grinding on each other. When the song ends, she looks dazed and satisfied. While he pulls his shirt down over his erection.

What is going on here? What have I missed in the past two months?

I want to cry so damn bad right now. Why would they do this to me? What did I do to deserve this type of disrespect from either of them? I feel a tap on the shoulder and look behind me. An older man is standing there.

Why did Keith have to do this to me? So he gets mad and chooses to play little boy games. Who does he think he is? I take a deep breath and realize that there would be no maybes tonight. I am done with him and her.

As I walk, back to the table with my soda and pretzels. I notice that Keith keeps his eyes on me the whole time. He was not sure if I had seen anything!

I thought that I knew him, but I did not have a clue about him. I ask the question, "How well we really know somebody?" Obviously, I did not know him well enough. To think I was prepared to give him my body tonight. Yeah he was smooth; smooth enough to break through my barriers. He almost had me, damn.

However, I do value myself. I am worth more than mind games and manipulation. I am not going to play my hand right now; I can wait with the best of them.

We stayed at the club until well after one in the morning. During the night Sheila kept asking what was going on and if I was okay. I assured Sheila that I was okay and having the time of my life. She and Ralph had stuck to each other the whole night. I was glad for her. I knew that she really liked him. I think that he wanted her just as much.

I noticed that whenever Ralph got up, and women approached him, he would back them off. Maybe he and

Sheila had a chance after all.

I played my part so well. The stupid, naïve, girlfriend without a clue. I danced with Keith even on slow songs. I let him squeeze me hard and kiss on my neck. Not once did I flinch or cringe away from him or try to smack his nasty face. But I wanted to, I really did!

We left the club in the wee hours of the morning. Keith, Mike, and Ralph asked if we wanted something to eat before going home. Everyone said sure. Therefore, we stopped at Bubba's tasty freeze. I am not sure how long Bubba's has been around.

I remember my grandfather buying us milkshakes on the weekends and on special occasions from this place.

With that said, I do know that it is older than I am. We could barely find a parking spot at Bubba's it was so packed. Little restaurants like this get all the business on weekends, especially in small rural areas. These areas are not like cities, which have ice cream shops and burger joints on every corner. Therefore, bubba's catches all of the revenue around here.

Bubba's is so busy that the men decide that it would be easier for them to go and place our orders.

"Sandra, what would you like?" Keith asked me.

"Keith, I just want a vanilla milkshake."

Candace looks and says, "That is all you want? What are you watching your figure or something?"

I think that I would love to punch her in the mouth. Look at her, trying to smother her laughter.

"Why would I need to watch my figure when I have people to do it for me? You know what they say about people always talking about and watching another? It's just envy."

"Sandra, I do not envy anyone," states Candace.

"Then why are you so worried about my milkshake Candace?"

I turned to Keith ignoring that bitch and repeat "I only want a shake, thanks."

"Sandra, come on and walk with me part of the way," Keith asks me.

"No, I will just stay here," I tell him.

Candace turns to Keith and asks if he needed help carrying the items back to the car. He looks at me as he tells her no he got it.

"Sandra, I will be right back with your shake," Keith says.

I stare at him. Do you feel something wrong playboy? I really hope you do. Does my body language say that it is over? I hope he is feeling the vibes flowing from me. It does seem like it too. He is nervous, keeps touching me, trying to look in my eyes.

Well screw him, because if he could do that with her. There is no telling what else they have been doing. That I know nothing about! Heck, if he could do that with someone I call a friend there is no telling how many girls on and off campus, he has cheated on me with. I have probably been the butt of many jokes and laughs.

I say to Sheila and Candace, I am going to go and stretch my legs. I just can't sit in that car pretending that I am cool with Candace.

As I walk around the cars in the parking lot. I hear someone calling my name. I turn around and see what used to be a close friend. His name is Calvin. We lived near each other in Meherrin. We were always cool with each other.

Calvin was also a friend of my ex, Blake. The end of that relationship was also the end of my friendship with Calvin. It ended on my part anyway.

I just felt that I would have to deal with Blake along with trying to stay in contact with Calvin. At the time, I did not want to do that. Therefore, I let a friendship slip away.

"Sandra, what's up? Long time no see," Calvin says.

"Calvin, it is great to see you."

"How are you and your family doing, Sandra?"

"I am fine Calvin, still doing this college thing. Thinking about job opportunities after I finish, you know. What about you, how are you doing?"

"Sandra, that is great to hear. As for myself, I am taking on-line courses in criminal justice through Lunenburg College."

"Calvin, I never knew you wanted to be a lawyer!"

"No not an attorney, Sandra. I want to go into law enforcement. Become a police officer and work my way up to detective, maybe even captain."

"Lord Calvin, we are something, right? I want healthcare, and you want law enforcement."

"I think we are looking to change the world a little at a time, Sandra."

"Calvin I know right? Only we can make our dreams come true."

"On a serious note, Sandra I know that you/we never talked about what Blake tried to do to you."

"Sandra, I knew that he was doping for the football team all along. You know Blake always said it was to get stronger and faster, he wanted to look good for the college recruiters."

I did not blame Calvin for what happened to me. I blame Blake, pure and simple. He is the one that hurt me.

"Calvin, Blake decided to take drugs, and he can say that he did it to get faster and stronger for the football team. Personally, I think he did it being selfish. He knew the side effects of taking steroids, he also knew the consequences if he was caught by the school."

"Sandra, I regret not saying anything. It may or may not have changed things, but I hate the fact that I will never know."

You know how you have flashbacks of the past or some incident that happened in your past? Well, I am thinking about the day that everything went crazy.

I had decided to breakup with Blake for real this time. I wanted the rest of my senior year to be stress-free. This would be no fluke or joke. I would not change my mind this time.

I decided to do it on a Friday. I had figured that early morning before we arrived at school would be best for him and me. When I think about it now, Blake was too quiet; not ranting, cursing, and shouting like he normally does when he would not get his way.

He made some threats of course, but I had prepared myself for that mentally. I even laughed when he said that I would be begging him to take me back by lunchtime. I was so proud of myself that day!

I did not back down or give in when his friends and my so-called friends, got in my face about it. I guess I did not have has many friends as I thought. I left school early that day. I just could not take any more harassment from everyone.

Non-friends telling me that I was wrong for it. That

tonight was a big game for them, and I was going to mess up his focus. I was raggedy, stuck-up, lucky to have him, a piece of shit, weak, dumb whore, and stupid bitch. I was all that and then some that morning.

I walked out of the school and hitched a ride to my grandparents' house. I love my granny. She knew something was wrong as soon as I came in. But she did not press it, she just let me go and lay down.

Unfortunately, Blake must have doped right before the game that night. The fool went out that evening and snapped so bad, they had to physically remove him from the field. I learned all of this after waking up in the hospital. Stupid me, I was the one to open the door for him at my grandparents' house. He proceeded to try to beat the life out of me that late night.

Well, at least, he tried I thank Jehovah every day

that my grandparents came home early and were able to stop him.

They saved my life that night. My grandfather said that when they walked in, he was just hitting me repeatedly with his fist. Pop stated that Blake was crazy that night. He looked as if he had snapped. When he got him off me, he cried and said, I made him do it. "DID I REALLY!"

I spent weeks in the hospital. Even longer after that healing my mind and spirit both were broken, not to mention parts of my body. My granny told me that it was by the grace of God that I survived that beating. I had so many injuries: a fractured jaw, broken ribs, broken nose, busted eardrum, a fractured pelvis, and a broken arm.

My granny said there was so much blood on my face that she thought I was gone already. However, my calm grandfather told her that it was my nose. That she needed to help me breathe. She kept pushing air into my body until the ambulance arrived.

Thinking about the past can cripple you. You have to find a way to move on. Deal with the emotions or situation, so that it does not cripple you in any way. My grandfather told me that. After he had realized that I kept having crying fits, would jump if someone walked up to me, and I could not stand to be touched.

Fear was my main emotion when I came home from the hospital. I was scared that it would happen again, that he would catch me somewhere and finish the job. My pocketknife became my best friend, sad to say, during this period in my life.

My grandparents' support was so crucial to my recovery. It was definitely needed when I found out that Blake would only get probation for what he did to me!

Blake's lawyer, parents, and friends claimed that the drugs made him do it. Of course: blame your behavior on the drugs.

He committed a crime and got off easy. I, on the other hand, had to learn to face my fears and deal with anxiety attacks. Over time, I got better and stronger. I would see Blake around town. As time went on, I stopped panicking when I saw him. I no longer turned and walked (at times ran) away.

"Calvin, you never really know a person. What Blake did was no one's fault but his. None of us will ever know if what he did was because of the steroids or not. I have come so far, that I refuse to go backward now."

"Sandra, do you forgive him then?" asked Calvin

"Honestly, I do not know Calvin. What I can tell you is that I am no longer a prisoner of fear. I do not dwell on it anymore, nor do I think about it."

"Sandra, how do we get over something like that?"

Laughing, I say to him, "How do we get over it?"

"You know what I mean, Sandra!"

"Calvin, if I can move forward after what was done. Then you need to as well."

"Can I have your number, Sandra? I would love us to stay in contact."

"No, I am not comfortable giving it out. Hey, you are home, so I know I will see you around. We can build our friendship from there Calvin."

"Okay, just stay in contact, please! My family would love to see you, Sandra."

As I walk back to Keith's car, I think about how this night, has been a night of new beginnings and reflections.

Ending

I am sitting beside this fool Keith, who keeps looking at me out of the corner of his eye. He needs to watch the road and not me. He really has nothing to worry about, I just plan to break up and move on. I want a clean break up between two adults.

Surprisingly, Keith takes his boys home first! As Mike gets out of the car, he comes up to the passenger window beside me.

"You good Sandra?" Mikes asks.

"Yeah I am fine, just tired that is all, Mike."

"Alright, try to get some rest then. I had fun with you all tonight."

"Mike so did I, and I will get some sleep. I plan to sleep in tomorrow."

"How you going to sleep in if you have to be at work in a few hours Sandra?" Mike said.

I look at him and smile "I am going to take a day for me."

Laughing with me, Mike says, "Okay, you wanna play with the big boys."

"Mike, since I never call out, I know that it will not be a problem. I should be good."

"Sandra, holla if you need something, okay?"

I never really realized it before, but Mike is a good person. He is tough, hard, what they call a thug. However, once you get to know him, you realize people are wrong about him. He is a good person/man.

I realize now that I have never heard him raise his voice in anger or fight. I am seeing him in a new light!

Grabbing his hand, I tell Mike that he is okay with me.

"Bet Sandra, Keith, girls I will catch you all later,"

Mike says to everyone.

I realize that we have to stop judging people based on that outside shell. You have to take the time and get to know someone. It's sad to say but I may be guilty of judging others on their appearance and what others say about them. I realize my perception of Mike was very different from who he actually is.

I wonder how many have judged me based on my looks or what I wear. I would bet a lot. The human mind can be so small at times.

As we drive off, Keith looks over at me.

"Sandra, is something going on that I should know?"

"What! What are you talking about Keith?"

"Mike and you were talking hush-hush, Sandra."

"Keith, we were not talking hush-hush as you put it!"

"Sandra, he even took your hand. I was just wondering if there was something that I needed to know."

"Keith, are you serious right now? Mike is a friend of yours, why would I go there?"

"Well, it does not look right when one of my boys is holding my girl's hand and whispering in her ear, Sandra."

I almost broke my neck whipping it around so hard. "So now we were whispering in ears, Keith?"

"Yeah Sandra," yelled Candace, "you two were whispering about something."

"Shut up Candace and mind your business," Sheila says to her.

"You shut up Sheila, Keith asked her first. I was just following and backing him up. He should know if his girl and best boy are plotting behind his back, right?" Candace said.

"Candace, take Shelia's advice and shut your mouth. Furthermore, mind your damn business and stay out of mine," I tell her.

I am so tired right now, mentally and physically. *I just wanna go home.*

"Keith, for your information I have no interest in screwing any of your friends."

"Sandra, I never said that you were going to screw Mike! I asked why he was holding your hand and talking low. What's the secret?"

"Ah, secret whatever, you are close to my place now, just drop me off here Keith."

"Wait a minute Sandra. I want to talk about this some more. No, I am not putting you off right here," Keith tells me.

"I do not wish to talk to you now or ever Keith!"

"Sandra, let me drop them off so we can go somewhere and talk."

"Keith, let me out of the car now, I am serious!"

"Sandra, Keith, what's going on? You both had been acting funny since before we left the club," Sheila asked.

"Sheila, it's nothing important," I tell her, "our stop is before Candace's and I just want to go home now."

"Sandra, Keith can let us out here and we can walk Candace half way to her place if that's what you all want."

"Sheila, I am not walking anyone home tonight. Keith can take her wherever."

"Sandra, hold on. That would not look right. I drop my girl off first, then take her friend's home?" Keith says.

"Sandra, that would not look right, girl," Sheila chimes in with Keith.

"Sheila, I could care less how it looks!"

How much longer? I just want out of the car before I break down in front of everyone. I am tired of trying to play the fool.

"Keith, I just want you to drop me off now. I am not asking again. By the way, when have you cared about how something looks, especially tonight?"

Sheila looks at me then at him and says to us both "Guys, what happened tonight?"

I look at Keith and say, "Ask Candace, and let me out of the car."

"Sandra, please, can we please talk about this?"

"Keith, I do not think that there is anything else to say, and I am trying to stay civil with you!"

He knows that we are done. Oh well, I cannot forgive what I saw tonight. There is no telling how much I do not know. If I let this go, there would be a next time. I can see it now. The sicko follows her into the woods while we're at a picnic, then tells me that I did not see what I saw, or that he does not know what he is doing.

Nope, I have no plans to end up like some of the girls I know. Miserable and screwing around because their friend is doing it. Yeah, the jokes and laughs are on me for now. That's okay, I am his loss: he is not mine. Plus karma is a bitch. He will get his.

Keith stops the car, and I jump, out without a word.

Sheila yells "wait up" and jumps out of Keith's car.

"Sandra, stop walking. What the hell happened tonight?"

Surprisingly, I did not cry, scream, or shout when I told her what I saw tonight.

"That low down, dirty dog. And I do not mean Keith.

How could Candace do this to you? We all have known each other for years, Sandra."

"I know, Sheila."

"You treated her like family, and she does this to you?"

"I know, I do not get it either Sheila."

"Damn girl, I am so sorry."

"Sheila, the grinding got me the most. They were grinding so hard on the floor I thought they should get a room."

"Sandra, those nasty bitches!"

"Sheila girl, she got to the end."

"What did you say? They grinded on each other until she finished, Sandra?"

"Yep, surely looked like it, Sheila. That's exactly what I said."

"Sandra, they both nasty as hell then Candace should have known better."

"I would have never done that to her, that I know Sheila."

"Sandra, just because you let her borrow your clothes and schoolbooks, should not have made her think it would be okay to borrow your boyfriend."

"I know. It's wild, isn't it Sheila?"

"Yeah, the trifling bitch crossed that invisible line, Sandra."

"I would not have believed it, had I not seen it for myself, Sheila."

"Sandra, I would have a hard time believing it now if it were not coming from you."

"Sheila, I was surprised, filled with disbelief at what I was seeing. I kept thinking, is he that mad at me for what Blake did? I also asked myself what I did to her, for her to allow it to happen."

"Girl get-out-of my face with that talk, we are all supposed to be grown-ups. If he was that mad at Blake, then he should have handled Blake and not hump bump with your friend!"

"Sheila, the only thing I can think is that they have been fooling around on me for a while. Candace may have met him before me."

"Would you want to know, Sandra? Think before you ask that question, the answer could hurt you more."

"Either way Sheila, I feel that they both played me."

"Sandra, I know. I see it in your eyes."

"Sheila, I wanted to share myself with him. If this had not happened, I would have slept with him tonight. Girl, I feel like such a naïve fool!"

"Hey Sandra, you want to know why I choose to wait to have sex?"

"Only if you really want to tell me."

"You know that there are seven of us."

"Yes girl, I know all your siblings."

"Okay well you know I love my mom, but I have to call it the way I see it. She was a ho, back in the day. I chose to save myself because I refuse to be like her."

"Sheila, stop. You do not say something like that about your mother."

"Sandra, please, I am honest. My father was my mom's best friend's, boyfriend."

"OOH shit! Aww Sheila...."

"Hush girl, let me finish. My siblings and I are all products of her cheating. I mean she always seems to want someone else's boyfriend or husband."

"Sheila, you do not have to say anything else."

"Sandra, I am trying to explain why I feel the way I do. My thoughts on him Sandra is that you will get over his betrayal and move on with your life. Hopefully you will use what he did to you and learn from it."

"I think I get what you're saying."

"Sandra, what Candace did to you was worse. You all's friendship may not rebound from this. What she did to you is similar to my own mother's actions. Sleeping with any man and not caring if it's your so-called friend's man or not."

"I do not know what to say."

"Sandra, my mom has fake friends. They all consider her to be a ho. They watch their men when she is around. They talk about her and you know they talk about her kids."

"What do you guys do about it?"

"We decided that we are not going to be like her. I do my best to make sure that my younger sisters are not out there. I even make sure the boys are not out there. I talk to my brothers and sisters about saving themselves for the right person."

"So you think that Candace did this because she is fast, and she wanted Keith?"

"I believe she likes guys that are attached to someone the bitch fast too. We both have fussed at her in the past, about messing with somebody's boyfriend. Like my mother, those are the ones that she wants so what we said fell on deaf ears. That's why I said that she is a ho."

"Sheila, I never thought she would do that to one of us."

"Sandra, every guy that looked at you around her

caused a comment to come out of her mouth. We both ignored it, saying she was just like that. Girl that shit was a sign. Seriously, just think about it!"

"What do you think I should do?"

"I know for me, that last night would have ended up in a fight. I would have whooped her ass."

"I know you would have. Girl come on let's get home, we can finish talking inside. In a few hours I need to call the clinic and put myself out for the weekend."

"Wow, now I know that you are hurt. Missing work, that is something you never do Sandra."

"Sheila, I know. But I do not think that it is a good idea to go in feeling this way! I feel depressed, and let down by him."

"You liked him Sandra, which is why it hurts."

"I honestly thought that he was a great person. He

did not try to play mind games or manipulate me as Blake did."

"Yes he did Sandra you just did not see it. He was obviously just that smooth with his game."

"Do you think more stuff will come out once people know that we are no longer together?"

"If he has done dirt, they are going to spread it all around. Just prepare yourself for what you may hear."

"I am just going to hold my head up and keep moving."

Who would have thought that Keith would turn out to be a worse than Blake? I thought that I went through some stuff with Blake. The manipulation and the added peer pressure had me ready to snap. Now, thinking about Keith, I have to admit it would have been worse.

After getting some much needed sleep, I called my

job then called my grandmother to let her know that I also would not be coming over today. I knew that I would hear about it later from my parents.

Nevertheless, I was just not in the mood to deal with my family's drama tonight. My grandmother was cool with the cancelation, but she warned me that my mother would not be happy. Point taken!

Motivation

My daughter. Yep, I said my daughter!

She looks so tiny and small. This little being is now my responsibility. She has a little round head, deep, dreary eyes, large lips, and the smoothest chocolate skin.

She smiled at me for the first time today. I am not sure if babies are supposed to smile so soon. Maybe it is gas she is only a few days old. I have a lot to learn about kids. I am so scared.

My daughter was born February tenth, four months later. We are packing up and leaving my grandparents' house. Our new home will be in Charlottesville, Virginia. I received a job offer from a nursing agency. It was not the coordinator position that I wanted. However, it gives me a chance to gain valuable work experience.

A coordinator position will come sometime in the future. For now, I am a proud administrative assistant. I still plan to get my degree. I have two more courses to complete before earning my Associates Degree. My plans have changed and adjusted to fit the needs of my baby girl.

My grandparents would prefer for me to stay longer or forever with them. I am going to miss them so much.

Nevertheless, I feel that it is time for Motivation and me to go. We have to leave sometime. I need to learn to survive on my own now. In my opinion, it is the only way for me to learn to be a good mother. I know that it will not be easy, nor am I expecting it to be.

I have two weeks to get Motivation and I settled before I start work. Yes, I call my daughter Motivation. Her legal name is Alyssa Alexandra Walts, however she is my Motivation to succeed, survive, and to thrive.

When I first found out that I was pregnant. I went

through a range of emotions. From complete confusion and bitter anger, to what else can happen to me now? I just wondered how much a person is supposed to take before they just snap. I have some strong shoulders.

The weekend I ended my relationship with Keith, I was attacked and raped by someone. Everyone thought it was my ex Blake, but it was not him. Yeah, I know that is a surprise. It was to me, I figured it was him as well. I just knew he was the guilty party. However, he had one hell of an alibi, for that long ago Saturday night.

Right after I saw him at the club that weekend, the police picked him up for driving under the influence and driving with an expired license. So Blake was in lock-up that Saturday night. But you know what? In the back of my mind I never really thought it was him. I just wanted it to be him. Maybe I wanted him to pay finally for what he did to me when we were kids.

As of this date, I have yet to learn the identity of my attacker. The coward wore a mask and gloves. The hospital and police were hoping to get a semen match since the condom the sicko had on burst.

The police did what they could with the information they had. I was informed that the samples they removed from me were run through their database. I guess the person did not have a record because they could not find him in their system. I did not understand that. Nevertheless, I can only go on the information given to me by the police. On the other hand, the sicko probably wears protection each time, and it holds up.

Well, that is how I ended up pregnant with my girl Motivation. On the other hand, that action could be just one of the reasons I ended up pregnant. The other is just plain stupidity on my part.

After the rape, I ended up in counseling again. I made the tough decision to keep the baby. At the time of my assault, the hospital could have given me something to terminate the pregnancy if I was pregnant. At the time I decided not to take that magic pill. I figured that the odds of ending up pregnant were not high. Stupid me, I was more worried about contracting a sexually transmitted disease.

I was released a few days later from the hospital. However, I did something stupid a few days later. It was as if I could not help myself. Stupid me, I had unprotected sex with someone. Yeah, I know you are asking why.

The only thing I can say in my defense is that I thought having sex on my terms would heal me. When old folks say that being young and dumb is a crime, in my case they were right. I made the whole situation worse.

Unprotected sex in a damn car of all places. What was I thinking? In reality, I was not thinking. At least not thinking the way a mature adult would think or handle the situation. Young and dumb should be tattooed on my forehead.

Well, I made the tough choice to keep my child. Several members of my family preferred me to have an abortion. I decided to be pro-me, take responsibility for my actions in this, and do the right thing. Of course, I had to discuss my decision with my grandparents. They understood. My grandparents were more open- minded about the situation.

They actually understood how my violation lead me to my decisions. That's not saying that they agreed with it, but they understood. Sheila was also, my rock during this time in my life. She and my grandparents were the only ones I told the truth. They knew and did not condemn me for what I did.

"Are you ready to go, girl?" Sheila yells coming up the stairs.

"I just have to carry this last bag downstairs."

"I am going to miss you, you know. I wish you and Mo were moving to Richmond with me instead."

"I know, I am going to miss you as well. But I want to go my own way."

"Shut up Sandra. You could still go your way there."

"Sheila, I got that job on my own, with no experience."

"I know, and I know it is a chance for a new start. But why can't you start over close to your family?"

"If you want the truth, I need to do this on my own.

Stand on my own two feet and know that I can make it."

"Oh, Sandra."

"I did not finish Sheila. I want to give my daughter more and be a better parent then what I got. I also do not wish to become a burden to my elderly grandparents. No, do not speak, I know they love me and want the best for me. But they deserve to enjoy their retirement without a grandchild and a great-grandchild on their backs."

"Sandra, you finish."

"No! I am not. I do not want them taking care of us. I want them to visit, and I visit them on occasions. I want them to go on those vacations together and not worry about my child and me. But most of all, I want them to know that they raised a strong and determined person, who will succeed in life."

"I am sorry Sandra. I did not get it. Well, I guess you

put me in my place!"

"Sheila, you are a meathead I am not trying to put you in your place. However, I need you to trust and understand that I know what I am doing."

"Well, it feels like you put me in my place anyway Sandra."

"I love you, Sheila, you are more than my friend you are family."

"I love you too, meanie."

"Has Mike started loading the truck yet?"

"Yeah, as I bring the stuff down, Mike and Ralph load it up."

"Oh that's great. I only have to grab, the rest of my items from the storage unit. We can do that on the drive out. I have a few more of Motivations, things to grab in here then we are done."

"Hey Sandra, are you taking any of the pictures in here with you?'

"I do not think so, I have pictures packed in my unit as well."

"Give me my goddaughter; I will hold her while you finish up."

"Hey Sheila, thanks!"

Sheila was a blessing. She was beside me from the beginning to the very end. The sad part about my decision to keep my child was the split between me and my parent's. Their reaction was not entirely unexpected. However, their decision not to speak to me anymore was a shock and blow.

They let me know never to ask them for anything and that they would not claim my child as a grandchild. Their distance has hurt me, but I will survive. Thirteen months after my ordeal. I have a child, a new job, and a new life. I could have fallen apart after what happened, but I was blessed and so covered with love, that I did not.

My rapist is still out there somewhere. I can tell you that my gut says that my ex Keith, is the guilty party. There was something so familiar about the person. The person's size always crosses my mind. I cannot put my finger on it. I cannot remember if I felt a jelly roll or not. However, I refuse to worry about that anymore as well.

I still get that nagging feeling whenever he comes around me. It's as though something is squeezing in the pit of my stomach. Well, that is how I got when he came to visit me during my hospital stay. How I get whenever we cross paths. His presence makes me so uneasy. I have told only Sheila about my feelings, why I think it was him.

I do not know why he came to see me. He acted as if

we were a couple. He told me that he would help me through my ordeal. I said no thank you, my friends and family got me. He even professed his love. Oh wow, love for real. Now that is truly laughable!

I heard from Sheila later during the year that he and Candace are officially a couple. This news comes as no surprise to me. I think they were cheating on me together all along. The way I look at it, if he did it to me, then me surviving is a slap in his face "No Woman No Cry" in my Bob Marley voice.

Mike was another visitor while I was in the hospital. During his visits, I learned that he wants to open a shop and detail cars and motorcycles. I asked him to be Alyssa's godfather. I was so happy that he agreed. Mike and Sheila will make good godparents.

Mike told me that he has already started to save up

for his shop. He and my grandfather talk a lot now. Mike says it helps him to have a man to talk to. I think that it is good for both of them. My grandfather is crazy about him. He keeps saying, "The boy is driven, and has ambition." He believes Mike will go far.

Sheila told me that Ralph and Mike both have left Keith alone. Yeah, that speaks volumes. She said that Ralph does not talk about why they left him alone. Yes, she and Ralph are finally a couple. I think that they will be good together. They both want the same things out of life.

Everyone knows that Sheila is moving to Richmond, Virginia to attend college at Virginia Union University. She will be working on her bachelor's degree and I am so proud of her. Ralph is relocating with her. He has gotten a good job. He still plans to return to school to finish his bachelor's degree as well. We all are moving on up!

Begin Again

I am tired, exhausted, hungry, and happy all at once. I finally have my keys in my hand to my new apartment. I love the fresh smell of the place. The walls look freshly painted, beige instead of white. New carpet on the floors, it actually fills thick. The kitchen is small, but I can still fit a small table in it.

"Oh wow look, Sandra, you have a microwave and a dishwasher already in the kitchen," Sheila said.

"Sheila, she is going to need both of those with this baby," my grandmother responded.

Sheila said, "Granny you are right about that, Sandra is going to need a washer and dryer as well."

"Sheila, check to see if there are hookups in that kitchen."

"Granny, the rent office told me that I could get both for a few extra dollars a month," I told her.

"Have you called them already to get one?" asked Sheila.

"Sandra, what are you waiting for?" my grandmother said.

"Granny, I wanted to see if my table would fit first," I told her.

"That dining and living area is huge; your table can go in that nook right there. Don't you agree, Sheila?"

"Yes ma'am, I agree," Sheila replied.

"Granny, Sheila, I will put the table in that corner, which is fine. We will be spending most of our time out here anyway," I tell them.

"Go call those people now while these menfolk's get this furniture in this house" granny orders me.

"Yes ma'am," I say to her. This is one conversation; I don't think I will win.

We have just finished moving all of my stuff in. At least I have two weeks to straighten this place up. I do not have a lot to do, thank the Lord. I just have to put our stuff away and organize the cabinets. Yep, and do it all with a four month old. But man, I am so happy for this next chapter to begin.

This key in my hand brings tears to my eyes. I know that my life and my daughter's life will not be easy. However, looking at this key in my hand right now gives me a sense of pride. I can do this! Yes, I can, yes I can!

In two weeks I start my new job, my daughter goes to a new babysitter, and our new life begins. I look over at my daughter in Mike's arms. She is a happy baby, already trying to hold her head up.

"Mike, do you want me to take her?" I asked him.

"No Sandra, I got little spitter!"

"I know you have to be tired, from moving my stuff, and now you are carrying this big spoiled baby."

"You and Motivation are my extended family you know. I will never be too tired to hold this kid," Mike says.

"We're crazy about you too. We love our Uncle Mike," I tell him.

"I did not like you moving out here, you know."

"Because you think I cannot do it, Mike?"

"Nah, you tough man, if anyone can do it you can."

"So Mike, what's the problem?"

"You got a lot of pride. Everybody's scared that when things get tough. That you will not ask for help!"

"I am stubborn and proud true, but this is no longer about me anymore. I have to think first about what is necessary for my child. Know this, I will ask for help when and if it's needed."

"Alright, Sandra, that is all I can ask. I will be up here, every so often to check on you two," Mike told me.

"I know, and I appreciate it," I said to him.

"You are like a sister to me and you know I take care of my family," Mike said.

"If I ever get in trouble, or need money I am going to call you all."

"Remember that you said that, Sandra."

Mike has turned out to be a great friend to me. More like a big brother who keeps it real and gives that unwanted advice that you do not want, but need.

"Mike, you ready to go?" my grandfather yells.

"Yes, sir," Mike says.

"Your grandfather, Ralph, and I are going to find a hardware store," Mike said.

"What for, Mike?"

"We are going to get new deadbolts for your doors and look at some new window locks too."

These men are a blessing to me. They love my child and me unconditionally. I walk over to my large bay window. As I stand here right now with my grandmother, Sheila, and Motivation looking out watching the sun go down.

I realize that I not only feel safe, but I welcome my new beginning. I am stronger than they know. I will not be, nor play a victim. "I am going to make it," I whisper to Motivation. She squeals, her approval. Good because now we can "fight and rise" and we will do it together.

MY MOTIVATION

Quote

"We don't have exoskeletons, but we can develop sensitivity to the energies around us and strengthen ourselves to be less victimized by those energies."

http://www.pure-spirit.com/more-animal-symbolism/611-butterfly-symbolism

About the Author

Kim loves different genres from urban classics; romance to science fiction novels. She has an MBA in Human Resources Management, but; her first love has always been writing. Besides reading and writing, you can find Kim outside getting her hands dirty in her garden.

She is an avid gardener, having earned a Master Gardener Certification from Virginia Tech. She volunteers her services to anyone who needs assistance with gardening.

Kim L.. Walton-Durham lives in Richmond, Virginia with her family. She is a lover of reading and quite often has a book in her face. She loves realism in books, especially in fantasy. She is a huge fan of Dean Koontz, Zane, Eric Jerome Dickey, and Stephen King.

Her wish is to have her stories reach out to the person reading; that they say or go WOW, I can relate.

Kim welcomes all feedback, negative and positive; because constructive criticism leads to growth. Kim promises that you will see improvement in her writing and story-telling skills with every single book she writes!

MY MOTIVATION

MY MOTIVATION